Sheep Out to Eat

Nancy Shaw

Sheep Out to Eat

Illustrated by Margot Apple

Houghton Mifflin Company   Boston

Also by Nancy Shaw and illustrated by Margot Apple:

Sheep in a Jeep

Sheep on a Ship

Sheep in a Shop

Sheep Take a Hike

Text copyright © 1992 by Nancy Shaw
Illustrations copyright © 1992 by Margot Apple

Library of Congress Cataloging-in-Publication Data

Shaw, Nancy (Nancy E.)
  Sheep out to eat / Nancy Shaw; illustrated by Margot Apple.
  p.   cm.
  Summary: Five hungry sheep discover that a teashop may not
be the best place for them to eat.
  RNF ISBN 0-395-61128-8   PAP ISBN 0-395-72027-3
{1. Sheep — Fiction.   2. Stories in rhyme.}
I. Apple, Margot, ill.   II. Title.
PZ8.3.S5334Sj   1992   91-38425
{E} — dc20   CIP
                              AC

Printed in the United States of America
WOZ 10 9 8 7 6 5 4

To Miriam and Nora Belblidia
— N.S.

To Graham Oakley, Monty Python,
and Marcy & Jack
— M.A.

Five sheep stop at a small teashop.

They ask for a seat and a bite to eat.

Sheep get menus. Sheep want feed.

They point to words that they can't read.

Sheep get soup. Sheep scoop.

Sheep slurp. Sheep burp.

Waiters bring them spinach custard.
Sheep add sugar, salt, and mustard.

Sheep take a few bites.
Sheep lose their appetites.

Waiters bring them tea and cake.

Sheep add pepper by mistake.

Sheep chomp. Sheep sneeze.

Sheep jump and bump their knees.

Table tips. Teacups smash.

Tea drips. Dishes crash.

Dishes break. Waiters stare.

Tea and cake are everywhere.

Waiters mop all the slop.

They ask the sheep to leave the shop.

Sheep pout. Sheep walk out.

Suddenly they look about.

Sheep crunch. Sheep munch.

The lawn is what they want for lunch.

Sheep smack lips. Sheep leave tips.

They'll stop again on other trips.